WITHDRAWN

P9-DVF-824

In memory of my much-loved sister, Julie, who unknowingly inspired this story —N.V.L.

For sufferers of dementia and the families who love them —S.G.

Text copyright © 2014 by Nancy Van Laan
Jacket art and interior illustrations copyright © 2014 by
Stephanie Graegin ◉ All rights reserved. Published in the United
States by Schwartz & Wade Books, an imprint of Random House
Children's Books, a division of Random House LLC, a Penguin Random
House Company, New York. ◉ Schwartz & Wade Books and the
colophon are trademarks of Random House LLC. ◉ Visit us on the
Web! randomhouse.com/kids ◉ Educators and librarians, for a variety
of teaching tools, visit us at RHTeachersLibrarians.com

Library of Congress Cataloging-in-Publication Data
Van Laan, Nancy.   Forget me not / Nancy Van Laan ;
illustrated by Stephanie Graegin. — First edition. pages cm
Summary: Young Julia comes to terms with the changes in her beloved
grandmother, whose Alzheimer's disease makes it hard for her to
remember people and things.
ISBN 978-0-449-81543-4 (hc) — ISBN 978-0-449-81544-1 (glb) —
ISBN 978-0-449-81545-8 (ebook) [1. Alzheimer's disease—Fiction.
2. Grandmothers—Fiction. 3. Memory—Fiction. 4. Old age—Fiction.]
I. Graegin, Stephanie, illustrator. II. Title.
PZ7.V3269 For 2014 [E]—dc23 2013007903

The text of this book is set in Belen.
The illustrations were rendered in pencil and ink washes
and then assembled and colored digitally.
Book design by Rachael Cole

MANUFACTURED IN CHINA
10 8 6 4 2 1 3 5 7 9
First Edition

Random House Children's Books supports
the First Amendment and celebrates the right to read.

forget me not

written by Nancy Van Laan & illustrated by Stephanie Graegin

schwartz & wade books · new york

I remember when Grandma was still her old sweet self, doing the things she had always done, exactly the way she had always done them.

She would still make my favorite fried chicken and biscuits whenever we visited.

She still set the table just so, with her napkins embroidered with forget-me-nots next to our plates.

And she still smelled like cinnamon and lilac when we cuddled up close.

When she called me Sally or Harry instead of my real name, Julia, I pretended it was a game that Grandma liked to play.

After she called out all my wrong names, I'd say, "No, silly, my name is Julia!"

Then she'd laugh and clap her hands and say, "Oh, silly me! Hello, bright-as-sunshine Julia!"

A little bit later, Grandma started forgetting all the things we'd done together, just the two of us. I'd say, "Remember the time we went berry picking and I fell into the prickly bush and got all scratched up?" or "Remember when we went to the zoo and I tried to climb over the fence to touch that huge elephant's trunk?"

"Why, no, you would never do such a thing," she'd say.

Once, Grandma went to the store and couldn't recall where
she had parked her car. When Uncle Harry came to her rescue,
she said, "I knew it was there the whole time. I just wanted to
see your handsome face!"

After she backed through the garage door, our family wouldn't let her drive anymore.

One night, Grandma invited us for dinner, but she
forgot to turn on the oven. We were about to settle for
just dessert, but her apple pie had a cup of salt in it, and
no sugar. We ordered takeout instead.

Not long after, I found Grandma's glasses in the refrigerator and a quart of tired old milk on her nightstand. She said she didn't do it, but who else would have?

Daddy arranged to have a nice lady cook and clean for Grandma. When Mrs. Hester showed up, Grandma swooshed her with a broom and called her a thief. So on cleaning days, we started to take Grandma for a long ride to nowhere special. She loved that.

"Smells like rain," Grandma would say sometimes on a perfectly clear day. "Better get out the umbrella." Then, a couple of minutes later, she would say, "Smells like rain. Better get out the umbrella."

And Grandma's head kept getting worse.

Twice, a neighbor called Mama and
told her to come pick up Grandma.

She'd gone shopping at Food Mart, but then

she couldn't remember where she was.

One awful snowy morning, Mrs. Hester found her in the garden wearing nothing but her nightie. She said Grandma was trying to pick forget-me-nots from underneath the snow, where they lay all crumpled and brown. Grandma seemed not to notice the cold.

When Mama and I got there, she didn't seem to notice us, either.

So I asked, "Mama, what's wrong with Grandma?"

She didn't say anything, just shook her head.

I asked again. "Mama, please?"

Finally, she answered.

"You know how some old people have trouble seeing or hearing? Well, some have trouble remembering—like Grandma. It's a sickness that nobody knows how to cure yet."

Mama drew me close, comforting like always. I clung to her like a twist of ivy and held tight.

"The next time we visit," she said, "Grandma won't be here.
She'll be in a place that will give her the special care she needs.
Others her age will be there, too. You'll see. It'll be okay."

It did not sound okay to me. I loved Grandma's house, with its front-porch swing and living room full of breakables she'd always let me play with. I knew she loved it, too.

But as it turns out, Mama was right.

Nearly all the time now, Grandma doesn't know who I am. Even so, I lean over to give her a big squeeze and smooth her white hair, soft as down. I just wish I could bring back whatever it was that made her eyes twinkle like candles on a cake.

Here's what I'm going to do.

As soon as the forget-me-nots burst into bloom, I'll gather enough to cover the quilt on her new bed. When she sees her bed all abloom, maybe Grandma will smile and clap her hands just like she used to.

It would make me feel good all over,
like the first day of spring.

31901055603114